FOURTH FLOOR, PLEASE

By

Bill Hunt

Edited by
Veronica Castle

Published by
Crimson Cloak Publishing

ISBN 13: 978-1-68160-047-5
ISBN 10: 1-68160-047-1

Table of Contents

This story is dedicated to my grandmother, Martha Bradley and my mother, Karen Hunt, Both are former employees of The Hub-- Steubenville, Ohio.

CHAPTER ONE

Eleven-year old Will Fellows lay flat on his back, looking up at the grinning face of his best friend.

"Gary, you can't just clobber a guy when he tries to go around you for a lay-up!"

Gary Thompson shrugged and extended a right hand to his fallen buddy. "Hey, I'm supposed to defend the basket, right? You have to admit: you didn't score."

"Stop fooling around," Will ordered, once again on his feet. "You know how the game is supposed to be played. Try-outs for Summer League are in one week. If you want to make it onto one of the teams, you are going to have to get serious about your level of play. You just aren't good enough yet!"

"Will is right," echoed Greg Marshall, who had been watching from the sidelines.

"If you don't step it up you're going to be sitting in the stands while Will and I have all the fun."

Gary dismissed the remark with a wave of his hand. "You guys are nuts for wanting to play in Summer League anyway! School is out in five more days. We have the whole summer in front of us and you guys plan to waste it on organized sports!"

"So, what do you want to do all summer?" Greg asked, defensively.

"Why do we have to 'do' anything?" demanded Gary. "Summer is made for goofing off!"

"All you ever do is goof off!" challenged Greg.

Will could sense the tension rising between his two friends, and he stepped between them. "Alright, guys! Knock it off! We have plenty of time this summer for sports and goofing around!"

"I knew you would see things my way," crowed Gary, triumphantly.

Will spun around to face his friend. "I'm not seeing things 'your way'! I said there was plenty of time to do both! Look: Greg and I are going to play basketball this summer. You want us to goof around with you—we want you to play ball with us. Is that so hard to understand?"

"I guess not," Gary admitted. "It's just that I'm not good at sports. I never have been. I'm four inches taller than anyone else in our class. You would think I would be great at basketball, but the fact is I'm clumsy! I trip over my own two feet just walking down the hall at school!"

"Which is why Greg and I are working with you," Will explained, struggling to be patient. "I can help you work on defense. Greg is a wizard when it comes to shooting."

"And, I'm better looking," quipped Greg.

Will stared at his friend. "What does that have to do with anything, Marshall?"

"Nothing at all," Greg said with a grin. "I just wanted to make sure you didn't forget that fact."

Will shook his head, retrieved the basketball, and once again instructed Gary: "I'm going to try the layup again. I want you to stop me without fouling me. Got it?"

Gary nodded, but said nothing.

Will began dribbling the ball at the half-court line. He made a few moves, as if avoiding invisible defenders then drove hard towards the basket where Gary waited. "Here I come!" Will shouted. Gary Thompson jumped just as Will began his lay-up and swatted the ball out-of-bounds with his huge right hand.

"That's how it's done!" Will shouted, enthusiastically. From the sidelines, Greg said nothing, but nodded approvingly.

"Hey, that felt pretty good!" said Gary, obviously pleased with himself.

"That's what we've been trying to tell you, Gary," Greg said. "You have all the tools to be a wicked shot-blocker. You could absolutely dominate the Summer League at the center position."

"Do you really think so?" Gary asked, still skeptical.

"Absolutely," said Will, emphatically. "You already have a decent hook shot. Greg is going to help you with your jump shot. You'll be unstoppable!"

"I still have trouble with free throws," Gary said. "Which one of you will help me with that?"

"I'm going to ask my great-grandma to do that," Will said, simply.

"*What* did you just say?" asked Gary and Greg in unison.

Will smiled. "I said my great-grandmother will help you with your free throws. She's deadly from the foul line. In fact, she's pretty good from almost any distance with a set-shot. Her jump shot isn't good anymore, though. She has a bum knee."

Greg Marshall shook his head in disbelief. "Will, your great-grandmother is like a million years old! You're telling me that she plays basketball?"

Will's grin broadened considerably. "First of all, Gigi is not a million years old. She's only 84. And, secondly, she does play basketball. At least she still shoots baskets. She'd beat all of our butts in a game of 'HORSE'."

Gary Thompson looked at Will with wonder in his eyes. "Your great-grandma's name is Gigi? Is she French or something?"

Will laughed. "No, she isn't French. Her real name is Edna. She came to live with us when my great-grandpa died. I was only 3 years old at the time. I couldn't say 'great-grandma'. She told me to call her G.G. instead, you know: short for great-grandma? Well, everyone else thought that her name really was Gigi! The nickname stuck! That's what everyone calls her now."

Greg was unimpressed. "You're trying to tell me that some 84-year old prune is better than me at 'HORSE'? I was the shooting champ of our school this year!"

Will was suddenly stern. "Watch your mouth, Greg. She may be old, but she's my Gigi and I love her!" He paused for a moment, then added, "I guess there's only one way to prove my point. Get your stuff: we're going to my house."

"Bring it on," Greg said with a smirk. "But, don't get mad at me when I make the old girl look stupid on the court!"

"We'll see," said Will, with just the hint of a smile. "We'll see."

CHAPTER TWO

It was a four-block walk from the playground to Will Fellows' house: a walk that Greg Marshall made much longer by making up a song about how badly he was going to embarrass Will's great-grandmother. *"Gonna beat old Gigi in a game of 'HORSE'; gonna make her feel bad, gonna make her feel worse!"* He looked over at Will. "You like my song?" he asked, with a mischievous grin.

"It'll never sell," opined Gary, before Will could respond. "First of all, the lyrics don't sound quite right. Secondly, you're an awful singer!"

Greg was unfazed. "You'll forget all about my singing when I totally toast the old girl," he boasted, spinning the basketball on his left index finger as they walked along. "Are you sure you want to go through with this, Will?"

"Funny you should ask that question," Will said, without turning to face Greg. "I was just about to ask you the same thing."

Greg Marshall stopped on the sidewalk. He tucked the basketball under his left arm and jabbed a finger hard into Will's chest. "I'm the best shot in our school, Fellows, and you know it! There are five letters in 'HORSE': I wouldn't be surprised if I beat your great-grandmother on five straight shots! At any rate, she's going down!"

"You care to make a bet on that?" Will asked, quietly.

Marshall sneered. "I'll be happy to take your money!"

Will shook his head. "No, we aren't going to bet money. You seem bent on making my Gigi look bad. If you beat her, I'll admit to everyone in town that you're the best shot. You'll also have the satisfaction of beating an old woman and making me look stupid for suggesting the contest. But, if Gigi wins ..." His voice trailed off into silence.

Greg eyed Will with suspicion. "If Gigi wins, what?" he asked.

Once again, Gary Thompson barged in. "If Gigi wins, you have to admit to all the coaches at the Summer League try-outs that you can't beat an 84-year old woman at basketball!"

Marshall roared with contemptuous laughter. "I'll take that bet in a heartbeat!"

The boys arrived at the Fellows' home a few minutes later. The two-story, white, wooden structure was similar in both size and value to the other homes in the small, well-kept neighborhood. Will's parents, Bill and Linda, were not home. Bill worked at a power generating plant a few miles south of town and Linda was off at one of her seemingly endless social activities. Gigi, however, was seated at the kitchen table, sipping coffee and reading the newspaper.

"Hello, Will," she said with a sweet smile. "Who are your friends, here?"

"This is Gary Thompson and this is Greg Marshall," Will said, indicating each boy, respectively. "Believe it or not, they've come to challenge you to a game of 'HORSE'."

Gigi put the newspaper aside. "Why would they want to do that, dear?"

Will grinned broadly. "I told them you were the best hoops shooter in town, that's why!"

Gigi shook her head, disapprovingly. "I've told you before, Will: bragging is not something we do in this family. It is unseemly."

"But, it isn't bragging if you can do it!" argued Will.

"Besides," Gigi continued, as though she had not heard Will, "I'm certain these young men have better things to do than pick on little old ladies."

Gary Thompson was horrified. "Oh, no, ma'am!" he stammered. "I don't want to challenge you. *He* does!" At this, Gary pointed an accusing finger at Greg.

"Is this true, young man?" asked Gigi.

Marshall suddenly looked like the 11-year old boy he really was. He gulped hard.

Very quietly he said, "Will said you were the best 'HORSE' player in town." Then, as if it were an afterthought, he added, "ma'am".

Gary Thompson could not resist. "He made a bet with Will that he could beat you!"

Gigi peered over her wire-rim glasses at the mortified Marshall. "Do you find satisfaction in beating senior citizens at sports?"

"Yes, ma'am, I mean, NO!! No ma'am, I don't like beating old people!" Small beads of sweat broke out on Greg's forehead.

"I didn't say 'old people', young man! I said 'senior citizens'!" Gigi snapped, reprovingly. Then, suddenly sweet again, she said, "Well, since you made the effort to come all the way over here, the least I can do is let you trounce me. Let me go change into some appropriate attire. I will meet the three of you out in the driveway in a few minutes." With that,

Gigi rose from her chair and exited the room without another word.

"I hope you're proud of yourself," Gary chided with mock seriousness. He was clearly enjoying Greg's discomfort.

"I didn't mean to upset her, Will. Just call the whole thing off!" Greg Marshall was more contrite than either boy had ever seen him. Still, Will was not willing to let him off the hook.

"You made the challenge. You made the bet. You have to go through with it."

Greg raised his right hand, and made a solemn pledge. "I swear, I'll go easy on her, Will. I won't embarrass her at all."

"Whatever," Will said with a shrug. "Just remember: if you lose, you have to admit to the Summer League coaches that an old woman beat you."

"Not an 'old woman'!" Greg said reprovingly: "A senior citizen!"

CHAPTER THREE

"Why do you think she's taking so long?" Gary wondered aloud as he looked at the rear door of the Fellows' dwelling. "We've been out here for 20 minutes already!"

"Be patient," Will advised. "You have to remember: Gigi is 84 years old! She doesn't move as fast as the rest of us."

"Well, I hope she hurries up," Greg countered. "I've been taking warm-up shots for fifteen minutes! I'm going to be worn out before we even start the game!"

The boys were standing on the wide, concrete apron that stood in front of the 2-car garage located behind the Fellows' house. The slab also served as the basketball court. The basket was located on the garage itself, centered above the double garage doors. The driveway was not large, but it could accommodate up to 6 players at a time: just right for Will and his friends.

"Here I am!" announced Gigi emerging from the back door of the house. "Sorry for taking so long!"

Gigi was wearing a pair of black, knee-length cotton shorts and a white, button-up cotton blouse that looked too large for her thin five-foot-two-inch frame. She also wore a pair of white ankle-high socks and an old pair of dirty tennis shoes.

"Do you like my uniform?" she asked the boys.

"It sure is different," said Gary, diplomatically.

"Well, it will have to do," Gigi said, flatly. "Remind me: what game are we playing, again?"

"You're playing 'HORSE', Gigi," Will said. "You and I play it all the time."

"I'm sorry, dear, I just get a little forgetful, sometimes."

'*HORSE*', for the uninitiated, is a game that can involve several players. The players first decide an order of play. The 'leader' attempts a challenge shot: if he makes a basket, then the next player up has to attempt the same shot. If he, too, makes a basket, then the next person attempts the shot. This goes on until a person misses the basket. The person who misses is given a letter from the word HORSE. When a person has accumulated all the letters, he is eliminated from the game. This goes on until only one person is left. That person is the winner.

In this contest, there were to be only two players: Gigi and Greg.

"Who is going to go first?" asked Gigi.

"It doesn't matter to me," said Greg.

Gary spoke up. "I think the gentlemanly thing would be to let the lady go first."

"Sounds good to me," Greg said. "OK, Gigi: you go first!"

Gigi took the ball and bounced it awkwardly a few times on the concrete. "I'm sorry, but I haven't had a chance to warm up yet. Do you mind if I take a few practice shots, Mr. Marshall?"

Greg grinned at her formal request. "Be my guest," he said, with a dramatic bow.

"Thank you," Gigi said with a slight curtsey. She took a stance under, and slightly to the right of the basket. She pushed the ball skyward and it clanged hard off of the iron, bouncing over near the flower bed. Will retrieved the ball for her.

"Thank you, Will," said Gigi, graciously. "I guess I'm a little rusty. I also may be a little too close to the basket. Let me step back a few feet."

This time, Gigi stood directly in front of the basket, about 6 feet back. Her shot missed the rim completely, bouncing off the top of the backboard.

Greg could not stifle his snicker.

Gigi shook her head. "I just don't seem to have it today," she said sadly. "We might as well start the game and get this over with." She took her place at the free-throw line and carefully lined up her shot. Suddenly, she tucked the ball under her right arm.

"I know what the problem is!" she announced. "I never could play ball with these glasses on! Will, would you mind holding them for me?"

Gigi walked over to where Will and Gary were standing. The boys had moved back closer to the house, in order to give Gigi and Greg plenty of room. She handed her wire-rim spectacles to Will. She then whirled around and, in one fluid motion, launched a beautiful, arching 23-footer that swished through the net without touching the iron.

"I believe it is your shot, Mr. Marshall," she said, simply.

Greg's mouth gaped open. "What the heck was that?" he gasped.

"That was a regulation NBA three-pointer, Mr. Marshall," Gigi said with a stone face. "As I said, it is your shot."

Greg looked at Will, panic in his eyes. "I've never tried a shot from that distance in my life!"

Will shrugged. "Well, there's no time like the present to give it a whirl."

Greg swallowed hard as he walked to the spot where Gigi had launched her rocket. He dribbled the ball nervously a few times, steadied himself and fired.

The ball fell 3 feet short of the rim.

"I believe that gives you an 'H', Mr. Marshall," Gigi said, icily.

Letters 'O', 'R','S' and 'E' followed in rapid succession, as Gigi dispatched Greg with five successive shots. None of Gigi's throws came from any closer than 15 feet, and she launched them from all sorts of impossible angles.

"Man, oh man! I cannot *wait* for Summer League tryouts!" crowed Gary. "Greg has to tell all the coaches that he was beaten by an 84-year old senior citizen! That's what the bet was!"

Gigi shook her head. "No one is going to tell anyone about this game," she said. "You heard me tell Will that boasting is unseemly. I meant that. It is equally wrong to embarrass someone in public. Do I make myself clear?"

"Yes, ma'am," Gary said, properly chastised.

Gigi turned her attention to Greg. "And, perhaps, you have learned a little lesson about cockiness today?"

"Yes, ma'am," Greg said, sheepishly.

"Good!" Gigi's glare suddenly softened and a twinkle returned to her eyes. "Now, inside with the three of you! I made some brownies earlier today and I see no need to let them go to waste!"

A few moments later, the four were seated at the kitchen table; a cold glass of milk and a small plate of fresh brownies before each of them.

"Where did you learn to shoot like that, ma'am?" Gary Thompson asked, his mouth full of brownie.

"Yeah," added Greg. "I would like to know that, too. You are crazy good!"

Will's great-grandma smiled. "Let's talk about something else, first. From now on, you boys can call me Gigi. As far as basketball is concerned, way back in high school I developed a crush on the captain of the basketball team. He was determined to play for a major college. He practiced all the time! The only 'dates' we ever went on were to the local playground where he shot baskets for hours on end! I had to learn to shoot just to be close to him. Eventually, we broke up: but I never lost my love of the game. By the way, he never played college ball." She paused to take a sip of milk before adding, "But, I did."

"You played college basketball?" Gary said, wonder in his voice. "What position did you play?"

"Point guard," Gigi said proudly. "I averaged 16 points a game. My specialty was a long-range shot from the top of the key. Remember: back in my day, they didn't have a three-point shot. If they had, my average would have been much higher."

Greg gave a low whistle of admiration. "That's impressive, Gigi! And, you are still shooting hoops at 84!"

"Never give up when you love something, dear," Gigi said earnestly. "Never give up on anything: or anyone."

CHAPTER FOUR

"No, Grandma! You got it wrong again! We go over this every week!" Linda Fellows was doing a poor job of hiding her frustration.

"But, I take two of these blue pills every morning!" Gigi protested. "I take two blue ones, a white one, a red one and that awful brown capsule that always gets stuck in my throat! If you don't believe me, you can call Dr. Moorhead. He'll set you straight!"

Linda struggled to maintain her composure. "Grandma, you still take the same dosage of pills, but the pharmacy has changed the look of the medicines. Instead of two blue pills you now take a gray capsule. You still take the white pill and the brown capsule. The red pill is now a blue pill, but you only take one. If you take two, you'll overdose!"

"What's wrong with these drug companies?" Gigi grumbled. "Don't they know they are confusing us old people? Are they trying to kill us?" She pushed the medicines across the table towards Linda. "You do it," she groused, "I'm tired of this foolishness!"

"It isn't foolishness, Grandma," Linda said wearily. "You have to take your medicine. And you have to know which medicine is which. I'm not always here to help you."

"That's true enough," Gigi said, sullenly. "You're gone more than you're here!"

Linda could take no more. "You know why I leave, Grandma? Because there are times that you drive me absolutely crazy!"

Linda regretted the words as soon as they left her lips.

Gigi recoiled at the words as if struck by a fist. For a moment, she and Linda started at each other in shocked silence. Then, very timidly, Gigi said, "I'm sorry you feel that way, Linda. I'll try my best not to trouble you." She quickly rose from her chair and exited the room.

Linda called after her, "Grandma! That's not what I meant!" But, Gigi was already headed up the stairs to her bedroom. A moment later, Linda heard her shut the door.

Gigi came back down a few hours later, right around lunch time. Linda was in the living room, reading a magazine. Gigi did not speak to her, other than to say, "I'm going to fix me something for lunch." Linda heard her rattle some pots and pans in the kitchen. A short time later, she heard the back door close.

About 20 minutes later, the kitchen smoke alarm began to chirp, loudly.

Linda rushed to the kitchen. It was foggy with white smoke but, thankfully, there was no fire. There, on the stove, was the source of the trouble: Gigi had put a pan of soup on to cook and then gone outside—leaving the liquid to boil dry. The smoke was coming from the scorched remnants in the pan.

Linda turned on the vent hood over the stove and opened some windows. Within moments, the smoke alarm ceased its piercing sound. Linda looked out the kitchen window and there was Gigi: working among the tomato plants in the garden.

Linda Fellows reached for her cell phone and dialed her husband.

"Honey, I told you not to call me at work unless it was an emergency," Bill chided.

"It is an emergency, Bill," his wife said wearily. "Your Grandmother had another one of her 'episodes' today."

"Oh, boy," Bill said. "What did she do this time?"

"She almost started a fire in the kitchen. She put some soup on and then went out to work in the garden. The soup boiled dry; the smoke alarm went off; the place filled with smoke and the whole house smells awful. If I hadn't been here who knows what would have happened? On top of that, we had another go-round over her medicine. Bill, I am scared to death that she is going to hurt herself!"

There was a brief moment of silence before Bill quietly asked, "What do you want me to do, honey?"

Linda took a deep breath. "I want you to call that new assisted living center we saw advertised on TV."

"You know she isn't going to want to go there," Bill warned.

"I don't know what else we can do, Bill," Linda said. "One of these days she really is going to hurt herself: or someone else."

There was another silence. Finally, Bill said, "I will call them as soon as I get off work this afternoon. I promise."

CHAPTER FIVE

Will always enjoyed the last days of the school year. This was the time when the homework ceased. This was the time when teachers stopped introducing new material. This was the time when textbooks were turned in and desks and lockers were cleaned out. And, Wednesday, the very last day of school, was the best day of all!

Will's school held an annual 'Field Day' on the final day. At noon, the entire student body assembled on the large field beside the playground for a picnic lunch. There were hamburgers and hotdogs; chips, cookies, fruit and soft drinks. Afterwards, the students had the freedom to join in any number of games, which were all supervised by the teachers. There was kickball, volleyball, flag football, Frisbee golf, foot races and, of course, basketball.

Will, Gary and Greg formed a team and entered the 3-on-3 tournament. The tournament was organized by the gym teacher, Coach Gregory. (Mr. Gregory, coincidentally, was one of the volunteers slated to coach in the Summer League.)

"This is your chance to show your stuff," Will said to Gary.

"Yeah, Thompson," Greg said with mock seriousness, "it's time to show the world we haven't wasted our time on you!"

The ordinarily meek Thompson surprised them both when he responded, "You guys hold up your end; I've got mine covered!"

A total of eight 3-man teams entered the tournament. Coach Gregory explained the format. "There is no way of 'seeding' this tournament according to power rankings, since none of you have played each other before. Therefore, I am going to be as fair as I know how. I have eight, folded pieces of paper in this can I'm holding. I want the captains of each team to come forward in a minute and take one piece of paper. On that paper is a number. That will be your team name and your 'seed' for the tournament. This is a single elimination competition. You lose a game and you are out! We will initially be able to play two games at a time: one on each half of the court. Captains, come get your piece of paper and return to your team!"

Greg Marshall was the captain of Will's team. He came back with a piece of paper bearing the number "3".

After a few minutes, Coach Gregory called for silence once more. "Alright, everyone has their team numbers! Here is how we are going to do this: Team 8 will play Team 1 on the court to my left. Team 7 will play Team 2 on the court to my right. When those games are over, Teams 6 and 3 will play on the left court; Teams 5 and 4 on the right! Mr. Gresham will referee the games on the right court and I will handle the games on the left. Games are played until the winner reaches 20 points and your team must win by 2! I will give further instructions as we get deeper into the tournament. Good luck, teams!"

"We don't play till the next game," Greg said. "Let's go talk strategy." No teams were allowed to wander too far from the court, but the boys managed to find a quiet spot near the swing sets.

Greg found a sharp stone and used it to scratch a rough diagram of the basketball court onto the dark surface of the playground asphalt. "These 'Xs' will mark our positions," he explained. "Will, you will be out front because you are our best ball-handler. I can move around on either side of the key. Gary, you take anything under the basket. You have to be our chief rebounder, too. And, let's pass that ball around! No need for anybody to be a ball-hog: we all know how to shoot. Take the shot you are most comfortable with, but don't force anything! Does everybody understand their assignment?"

Will and Gary both nodded.

By the time the trio made their way back to the court, the first games were winding down.

Teams 8 and 2 would eventually win their respective games. The boys noticed that, though neither team was overly impressive, Team 2 had a guard who was an excellent ball-handler.

"Teams 6 vs. 3 and 5 vs. 4: you guys are up next!" Coach Gregory shouted.

Will, Gary and Greg took the court and quickly sized up the competition. Will and his friends were just finishing their sixth grade year. Their opponents were three boys closing out 5th grade. All six boys proved to be decent players. However, the additional year of experience for Will and his buddies proved to be too much for the younger players. The final score was 20 to 12. Over on the other side of the court, Team 5 beat Team 4 by a margin of only 2 points.

The semi-final matches pitted Team 2 against Team 5 on the left side of the court. On the right side, Will's team faced the boys from Team 8.

Will and company discovered that the players in this contest were more evenly matched. The only advantage

Team 3 possessed proved to be Gary. His 4 inches of extra height made the difference. With the game tied at 18, Thompson grabbed the rebound off an errant shot by Will and laid it back in for the 20th point.

On the left-side of the court, team 2 handily dispensed with Team 5 by a margin of 20 to 14.

Coach Gregory blew his whistle and called for quiet. "It is time for our championship game! Would teams 2 and 3 come to center court, please?"

The six players stood in a loose circle around Coach Gregory as he gave his final instructions. "I would like the two captains to step forward, please."

Greg, along with Pete Gaudio, the fifth-grade ball-handler from Team 2 stepped forward.

Taking a quarter from his pocket, Coach Gregory said, "Mr. Gaudio, I want you to call 'heads' or 'tails' when this coin is in the air." The coach flipped the quarter skyward.

"Heads!" Pete shouted.

"Heads it is!" declared the coach. "Would your team like the ball first, or would you like to choose left or right side of the court?"

Gaudio did not hesitate. "We want the ball first!"

Turning to Greg, the coach asked, "Which side, Mr. Marshall? Left or right?"

"We want to play on the right side of the court, sir," Greg said.

"Very good," the coach said. "Gentlemen, this game will decide the 3-on-3 champions for this school year! We have individual trophies for each member of the winning team, and medallions for the runners-up. Play hard and play fair! Let's have a good game!"

The teams took their places and, when Coach Gregory sounded his whistle, the game began.

Along with fifth-grader Gaudio, Team 2 was comprised of sixth-graders Kirk Kendor and Allen Key. Kirk and Allen were not known for their shooting skills, but both were aggressive players on the court.

Pete Gaudio took the initial, in-bound pass from Key, skirted quickly around Greg Marshall and pulled up for an easy 8-foot jumper to put his team ahead 2-0.

Will's team soon evened the score, but they were more methodical in their approach: passing the ball around several times before Greg Marshall was able to score an easy lay-up.

The game went on for several minutes with neither team able to get more than a 2 point lead at any time.

In half-court basketball, whenever a team misses a shot and the opposing team rebounds, the ball must be taken back to the foul line before that team can score. With the game dead-locked at 18, Gary Thompson grabbed the rebound from a Kirk Kendor miss; spied Greg Marshall at the top of the key and flung the ball towards him.

"Shoot it!" Thompson shouted.

Greg caught the ball. There was no time to dribble: Pete Gaudio and Allen Key were both bearing down on him. He quickly launched an arching rainbow of a shot that banked off the backboard through the hoop for the win.

Gary and Will jumped up and down and pounded on Greg's back in jubilation.

"How did you do that?" Gary asked. "You couldn't hit anything from that distance the other night at Will's house!"

Greg grinned sheepishly. "I know. I was so embarrassed by Gigi that I've spent two hours every day since at the playground practicing until I got it right!"

Will was exultant. "I'll make sure I tell Gigi about that when I get home!"

Coach Gregory's whistle sounded a final time. "Would the winners and runners-up please join me at center-court!"

The six players gathered in a loose circle around the coach.

"Gentlemen, that was some great basketball out there this afternoon! I'm proud of each one of you. And, I would like to personally extend an invitation to each of you to be part of the Summer League. We're going to add something new to our format this year: along with our regular style of 5-on-5 play, we are going to have a 3-on-3 tournament. It would be a real treat to see your two teams compete against each other again."

Pete Gaudio raised his hand. "Are you saying we don't have to try out for Summer League? We're already in?" he asked, quizzically.

Coach Gregory nodded. "That's right. The other Summer League coaches gave their permission for me to offer an exemption to the top two teams of this tournament. So, what do you say, boys? Are you in?"

All six young men shouted their hearty agreement.

"Excellent!" said the coach, with a broad smile. "Now: you will be divided up along with the other kids for 5-on-5 play, as always. But, one day each week will be allotted for 3-on-3 practice. The whole Summer League program runs from June 5 to July 18. We play every Friday and Saturday evening during that time. The 3-on-3 tournament takes place Friday and Saturday of the final weekend. I can't wait to work with you fine young men! Now it is time to pass out the awards."

Walking home from school later that day, Will's spirits could not have been any higher: school was out, his team had won the tournament, and he held the first real trophy of his life tightly in his left hand. All was right with the world!

That is, until he approached his driveway. Both of his parents' cars were there (that was not unusual: Wednesday was Dad's day off and Mom had no social engagements until evening.) But, the large, black sedan with the words "Glenhaven Assisted Living Center" emblazoned on its side was definitely out of place.

CHAPTER SIX

Will quietly opened the front door and peeked inside. There was no one in the living room, but he could hear voices coming from the kitchen. He slipped inside and softly closed the door behind him. He took a few more steps, so that he could see into the kitchen ... all the while hoping he would not be seen.

His father was seated at the head of the table, facing the living room. His mother sat at the other end. Gigi was seated on the right side of the table, in her usual chair. Across from her was a smiling, bald man in his mid-50s. He was holding up some kind of brochure or book so that Gigi could see it. Gigi was not smiling: in fact, she looked frail and slightly dazed.

At that moment, Will's father noticed him. Without saying a word, he pointed "*up*", indicating that Will was to go upstairs to his room. Will began to protest, but Dad put a finger to his lips and again gestured "*up*"!

Will complied, reluctantly. Once in his room, he tried to figure out just what was going on downstairs. He had never heard his parents talk about assisted living before. And, by the look on her face, this could not possibly be Gigi's idea.

Will was still mulling the whole thing over when, about 20 minutes later, he heard a car door slam and an engine start.

He looked out of his window just in time to see the black sedan pull out of the driveway.

A moment later, there was a gentle knock at his bedroom door.

"Come in," Will said.

His father walked inside.

"So, how was the last day of school, Sport?" dad asked with a forced smile. Will could tell something was very wrong. He ignored the question and asked his father directly.

"What was that man doing here?"

"Sit down, son," his dad said, pointing to the bed. "We need to talk."

Will obeyed. His father sat down beside him. Will could feel a knot beginning to form in his stomach.

"Gigi is going to be moving out in a few weeks," his father said, quietly. "She's going to live at the Glenhaven Assisted Living Center."

"But, why does Gigi want to leave?" Will asked, clearly puzzled. "Isn't she happy here?"

"She's very happy, Will," dad said, gently. "That isn't the issue. Gigi has been having problems lately. She forgets things."

"Lots of people forget things, Dad," Will said, defensively, "especially old people. Everybody knows that! You don't ship them away because of that, do you?"

"It isn't like that, Will. Gigi doesn't just forget dates and places. She forgets important things. She forgets what medicine she is supposed to take and when she is supposed to take it. A couple of weeks ago, she took twice as much as she was supposed to. Fortunately, it didn't hurt her: but, next time it could."

"Then, why don't you and Mom help her with the medicine?" Will pleaded.

"We've tried, Will, but she still makes mistakes. And that isn't the only problem: a few days ago, she put on a pan of soup and then went out to work in the garden. The soup boiled dry and we almost had a fire in the kitchen. If your mother hadn't been here, the whole house might have burned down! Gigi is going to move to a place where she'll still have plenty of freedom; but there will be people there to watch her 24 hours a day."

Will was silent for a moment. Then, softly, he asked, "How far away is this place?"

"It's about an hour away," his father answered.

"When will we get to see her?" Will asked, his voice barely above a whisper.

His dad was non-committal, "We'll go see her from time to time."

Will could bear it no longer: the rising wave of grief burst through its dam. "No, we won't!" he sobbed, angrily. "We'll never see her! You work all the time and Mom is always gone! When would we have time to go?"

Will's father put an arm around his son in an attempt to console him, but Will tore himself away. He fled the bedroom, raced down the stairs and exited out the backdoor. The first object he encountered was his basketball. Will kicked it as hard as he could. The ball ricocheted off the garage door with a loud "bang!" The ball bounced away, eventually rolling to a stop in Gigi's flower garden.

The sight of the ball lying in the midst of the brightly-colored flowers caused all the anger to drain out of him. It was replaced with a feeling of deep sadness. He retrieved the ball and spent the next few hours randomly shooting baskets as he tried to calm his mind.

The sun was beginning to set when he heard the back door open.

It was Gigi.

"I understand your Father had a talk with you earlier," she said quietly.

The tears began to flow again as Will said, "I don't want Mom and Dad to send you away, Gigi!"

She smiled at him. "No one is sending me away, Will. Your parents and I made the decision together."

"It won't be the same without you here," Will said, the hot tears burning his eyes.

"Well, that's change, Will," she told him. "Nothing stays the same forever. You learn to adapt. I didn't think I could ever go on after your great-grandfather died–but I did. I miss him terribly, but I don't let missing him ruin my happiness. Besides, I'm not going to be that far away."

"You'll be an hour away," Will reminded her, sadly.

"Oh, that's not so far," she said brightly. "Besides, in five more years you'll be driving. I suggest you take your Mother's car when she isn't looking and come visit me."

Will laughed.

"So," Gigi continued, "we will have no more tears! We'll enjoy the remaining time we have together and take whatever adventures there may be after that! Now, hand me that basketball!"

And that is how the two of them spent the rest of that Wednesday evening: shooting baskets until the sun set and the fire-flies appeared.

CHAPTER SEVEN

"Will? Will? Are you up yet, honey?" His mother's shout, wafting up from downstairs, roused Will from his slumber. He looked at his alarm clock. It was 8:30 am, Thursday, June 4th: the first day of summer vacation.

"I'm awake!" shouted Will, sleepily. "What do you want?"

"Would you come down here, please?" his mother called. "I want to talk to you about something!"

"Gimme a few minutes to get dressed," Will hollered.

About ten minutes later, Will entered the kitchen. His mother was seated at the table.

"What's up?" he asked.

His mother pointed to the front page of the morning paper. "Read that," she ordered.

Will glanced at the headline, then turned to his mother and asked, quizzically, "You want me to read about the new sewers the city is putting in?"

"No, silly!" his mother said, with a frown. "Read the story *under* that one: the one about the store."

Will turned his attention back to the newspaper, and read the brief, three-paragraph blurb.

"Isn't this the place where Gigi used to work when she was younger?" he asked, without looking up.

"Yes, it is," his mother replied.

"The article says they are going to tear it down. Why is it important for me to know that?"

"Will," his mother said, with slight irritation, "didn't you read the *whole* article? It says the management of the store is going to hold a special reunion there for its old employees! I think Gigi would like to go, don't you?"

"So, let her go!" Will said. "There is nothing stopping her. The article says the store will send a bus to pick up any interested former employees: all they have to do is call the number listed in the paper!"

"Do you remember the conversation you had with your Father last night? He told you Gigi was having memory problems. I think it would be good if she had a chaperone for the reunion."

"So, why don't you or Dad take her?" Will asked.

"The reunion is tomorrow. Your Dad works all day and I'm hosting Card Club here at the house. You are the only person who is free to go!"

"But, I'm not free," Will argued. "Gary, Greg and I are getting in some last minute practice today and tomorrow before the start of Summer League."

"I thought you said you didn't have to attend Summer League tryouts," his mother reminded him.

"We don't have to attend them," Will agreed, "but, since the season starts this Saturday we want to be really ready!"

Will's mother put her hands on her hips. "Will Fellows, your great-grandmother worked at that store more than half a century ago! She probably only has a few friends from there that are still alive! Are you going to deny her the chance to see them one more time?"

"I guess not," Will said, after pondering the question. "So, how much of the day will this take up?"

Will's Mother smiled, "That's what I wanted to hear! The article says that the bus would pick everyone up no later than 11:00 and have them home no later than 5:00. It also says that a lunch would be provided, so you won't starve to death."

"Has Gigi read the article yet?" Will queried.

His Mother shook her head. "No, she has not read it. I wanted to ask you about it, first. She's out in the garden: I think you should tell her."

Will nodded and headed for the back door. Gigi was pulling weeds, "Good morning, Gigi!" he called, cheerily. "Do you have a minute?"

Gigi stood and wiped the sweat from her forehead with her gloved hand. "Whew! Yes, I'll be happy to take a break! What's on your mind this morning?"

"You used to work at The Hub, didn't you?" Will asked.

"Oh, yes, dear–but that was a long, long time ago!"

"Well, they are tearing the place down in a couple of days."

Gigi shook her head sadly. "I hate to hear that! It was such a wonderful place back in its day! The store went out of business about twenty-five years ago, but I always hoped, somehow, that someone would use that magnificent old place for something worthwhile! All that's in there now is a bargain furniture store on the first level."

"Well," resumed Will, "the old management is going to have a reunion there tomorrow for any of its old employees that want to come. Would you be interested in going?"

"Oh, that would be glorious!" Gigi exclaimed, clapping her gloved hands together. "I have some old friends that I'm pretty certain are still alive, but I have lost contact with them. Perhaps they will be there!"

Will grinned, pleased at his great-grandmother's excitement. "I'd be happy to go along with you, if you would like," he offered.

Gigi beamed. "I would love it!" she said. Then she frowned, "but how do we get there?"

"The management is going to send a bus to pick up anybody that wants to go. All you have to do is call the number in the newspaper article."

"Well," said Gigi, as she strode to the house, "let's just call that number right now!"

About ten minutes later, Gigi set the phone aside. "We're all set!" she told Will, proudly. "The bus should pick us up here around 10:45!"

"Sounds good to me," Will said. "I have to make a couple of calls myself now."

"Oh? Who are you calling, dear?" Gigi asked.

Will grinned. "I have to tell Gary and Greg that I can't practice tomorrow: I have a date!"

CHAPTER EIGHT

"Our chariot is here!" Gigi announced with fanfare. She grabbed her purse and headed outside. Will followed her out the door. When Mother had said Gigi's old employer was sending a bus to pick them up, he assumed she meant one of those big, gleaming tour buses he occasionally saw on the interstate. What greeted him was an old, beat-up school bus rented from one of the larger churches in town.

"This thing is a wreck," Will whispered as he helped Gigi up the steps of the bus.

"It will do just fine," she whispered to him.

The bus was not crowded: there were only a handful of elderly passengers scattered throughout the vehicle. Gigi took a seat on the left side, near the front, by a window. Will slid onto the seat beside her.

"There's no air conditioning," Will noted.

"That's why we have windows," Gigi answered cheerfully, sliding hers open. "Besides, it's a nice day: I'd rather feel the breeze."

The bus driver turned and announced, "You are my last pick-up. Next stop: the big city! We should be there in about half an hour!"

"Big city: yeah, right!" Will thought to himself with a smirk. The old steel town where they were headed was a shadow of its former self. The mill had closed 20 years before he was born. The population of the town, once 50,000, was now barely 15,000. The formerly bustling downtown was now a dismal stretch of shuttered storefronts and decaying buildings: a haunt for street gangs and drug dealers. It was a dangerous place.

Will was glad he lived in the suburbs.

"It will be nice to see the old store again," Gigi said suddenly. "I loved working at The Hub!"

Will wrinkled his nose. "That's a weird name for a store."

Gigi nodded slightly. "That's true: but the word 'hub' means 'center'. There was a time when The Hub really was the center of town. Oh, it was a grand place!"

Will was unimpressed. "A store is just a store," he said.

"Oh, so suddenly you're an expert, are you?" said Gigi with faked indignation. "The Hub wasn't just a store: it was a destination! People got dressed up to go there. It was a huge building: four stories high and almost the size of a city block. There was a Paramount movie theater next door and people who came to the city often made a day of it: they would shop at The Hub during the day and take in a show at night. The store also had a very nice restaurant on its mezzanine."

"On its what?" Will asked. "I've never heard that word before."

"On its mezzanine. It's hard to explain, but basically, a mezzanine is a floor between two stories of a building. Perhaps I can show it to you when we get there. Of course, the restaurant is gone. That's a shame, too. To this day I've never had a better hamburger than what they used to serve there."

"What did you do at the store, Gigi?" Will asked.

"I was a cashier on the fourth floor. Oh! The fourth floor was the best floor in the store!"

"What did you sell there?"

"We sold bedroom furnishings and curtains. The Hub was what was called a department store. You've been to a mall before: at a mall, every shop is a specialty store. There are book stores, clothing stores, shoe stores and so on. A department store sells all of those things, and more, in different areas—or departments—of the building. At The Hub, tools and hardware were sold in the basement. On the first floor you could buy cameras, televisions, shoes and clothing. The mezzanine restaurant was between the first and second floors. On the second floor you could buy appliances and kitchenware. Third floor was furniture; I've already told you what we sold on the fourth floor. The fourth floor was definitely the best place to be."

"Bedroom furnishings and curtains are that exciting, huh?" asked Will teasingly.

"No, silly!" said Gigi, giving him a playful punch on the arm. "What made the fourth floor special were the people I worked with: they were the best. And you couldn't beat the fourth floor at Christmastime."

Something in Gigi's tone made Will ask, "What was so special about Christmastime?"

Gigi turned in her seat so that she was facing Will directly. "The Saturday after Thanksgiving, each year, there was a huge Christmas parade in town. Of course, at the end of every Christmas parade, there is Santa Claus. Well, Santa always came directly to The Hub immediately after the parade. There were Santas at other stores in town, but only The Hub had the *real* Santa Claus! Each year we turned half the fourth floor into a magical toy land for Santa. I forgot to mention that we also sold toys on the fourth floor, so it was the most logical place to put Santa Claus. Oh, how I wish you could have seen what the store looked like back in those days!"

For the next 15 minutes, Gigi regaled Will with stories of Christmases past at The Hub. Will was mesmerized.

"OK, folks, we're almost there!" The voice of the bus driver pulled Will back to reality. "Just a few words of advice before we stop," the driver continued. "This is a pretty rough part of town: for your safety, the management has hired policemen to guard each entryway. There are also security guards inside the store. We ask that you don't venture outside and that you only use the main entrance. I'll be back to pick you up at 4:30. Have a good day and stay safe!"

The bus began to slow. Will turned and looked across the aisle, out the window on the right side. The Hub was coming into view. Based on Gigi's stories, Will expected to see a brightly lighted, gleaming, white palace. What he saw was a smudged, ivory-yellow building with a series of bleak, empty display windows. Some of the windows had cracks in them. One even had a bullet hole in it. A few windows had been plastered with signs that said, "Big Blowout Sale Today!" Gigi reminded him that a discount furniture company rented the first floor of the old store, and they were holding one final sale before the building's demolition.

"Well, we're here!" Gigi announced, gripping Will's arm. "Isn't this exciting?"

Out of all the words Will knew, 'exciting' was the very last one he would have chosen.

CHAPTER NINE

"Welcome!" said a short, sweating man who held the door open for them. "Are you here for the furniture sale or The Hub reunion?"

"We're here for the reunion," Gigi replied cheerily.

"Then, after you enter the store, you will want to turn to your right," the man said. "You'll see the signs. Have a nice day!"

"Thank you very much," said Gigi, striding off at a brisk pace. Will hurried to keep up with her.

"What's the hurry, Gigi? We've got all day!"

Gigi ignored him. Apparently, she had caught sight of some people she knew because she suddenly called out, "Martha! Eloise! Hello, girls: it's me!"

Two elderly women standing near a table at the far side of the room turned towards them.

"Is that you, Edna?" a woman wearing a dark blue dress.

"Of course it is, Martha!" said her companion. "I'd recognize that voice anywhere!"

Within moments, the three ladies were chatting away as only the best of friends know how. Will felt uncomfortable and out of place. Gigi noticed and grabbed him by the arm.

"Girls, this is my great-grandson, Will. Will, this is Eloise, and this is Martha."

"It is nice to meet you," Will said, feeling more uncomfortable with each passing second.

"My, he's a tall one," said Eloise, admiringly. "He didn't get that from your side of the family, Edna!" The ladies laughed. Young Will now felt embarrassed as well as uncomfortable. He was relieved when Gigi said, "Will, I know you don't want to hang around with a bunch of old women all day. Why don't you go explore the store? I'm afraid only the first floor is open, but you might find something that catches your interest."

"Thanks, Gigi," said a grateful Will.

"There's a lunch table just around the corner," Martha said. "It isn't much. Just some sandwiches, chips and soda - but it should fill you up."

"Thank you," said Will. "What time do you want me back here, Gigi?"

"We're supposed to catch the bus at 4:30, so be back here by 4:15. And, whatever you do, don't leave the store!"

"Yes, Gigi: I promise!" With that, Will Fellows set off to explore.

He spent the first half hour looking at the items in the furniture store. As noted earlier, the defunct Hub was located in a now-decaying part of the city. Many of the people who lived there were poor and the discount store catered to their needs. The furniture was cheaply priced and, unfortunately, cheaply made.

"I wouldn't want any of this junk," Will said to himself. He soon tired of looking at the furniture and turned his attention to the building itself. The Hub had ceased operations more than a quarter of a century before. The majority of its furnishings had been stripped away and the paint and plaster were in an advanced state of decline. Still, it was evident that, at one time, The Hub had been a magnificent structure.

The first thing Will noticed was the sheer size of the place. The ceiling was a good 20 feet above the floor. It was supported by a series of huge columns scattered throughout the building. This gave the floor a very 'open' feel and a classic Greek appearance. Contributing to that impression was the floor, which was marble. Originally white, the floor now was dingy yellow due to many layers of aging floor wax.

Will decided to explore the store in a methodical manner. He went back to the main entrance, which was located on the south-facing wall, and began walking the perimeter of the building in a counter-clockwise fashion.

Along the east wall he found signs marking the "Shoe" and "Electronics" departments. These signs were painted on the wall itself and were difficult to read, owing to a combination of fading and peeling paint. He could make out the top of another sign, but could not quite read what it said, due to the fact that a large wall of boxes blocked his path. He made a mental note to return later and get behind those boxes, if he could, to read the sign.

Along the right side of the north wall he came across a short staircase. It went up about 10 feet to a landing between the first and second floor. He realized, with satisfaction, that he had found the mezzanine Gigi had spoken of earlier. Looking quickly left and right, to determine that no one was watching, Will climbed the stairs.

The mezzanine, according to Gigi, was once home to The Hub's restaurant. Will was surprised at how small the place was. A small table and a single chair stool against a far wall. By rough calculation, Will determined that the restaurant could not have seated more than thirty diners at one time.

Behind the long-discontinued lunch counter, he found a yellowed piece of paper which bore the restaurant's menu. Will marveled at it: a meal of a burger, fries and a soft drink would only have set him back $2.15! Carefully, he folded the menu up and slipped it into the pocket of his slacks.

Unable to find anything else of interest on the mezzanine floor, Will descended the stairs and resumed his exploration of the ground floor.

Along the far left side of the north wall he discovered a staircase that apparently led to the other levels of the store.

The west wall held a few more signs ("Camera Department" and "Men's") as well as a partially opened door that proved to be the entrance to one of the display windows. Will peered through the door, but twenty-five years of accumulated filth kept him from seeing through the window.

He looked at his cell phone: it was 1:30. He had done all the exploring he could and he still had nearly three hours to kill. He decided to go back to the east wall and have a look at the sign behind the boxes.

Upon arrival, he discovered that boxes belonged to the discount store. Even with the sale, it was evident that a great number of items would be left over. The boxes were to transport these items to their next location - before the demolition began.

It was an impressive stack of boxes: nearly 30 feet long, 10 feet deep and 10 feet high.

Will stepped around the left end of the stack and read the sign that had largely been hidden from view. It said "Elevator".

And, indeed, there was an elevator there. At least there was the *door* of an elevator.

It was closed, of course, and a hand-lettered, cardboard sign was taped to it which read "Out of Order." Will moved closer, so he could inspect the sign. It appeared to be very old. "I'll bet this elevator hasn't run in 25 years," he said to himself, touching the sign.

As soon as Will touched it, the sign fell from the elevator door. He picked it up and examined the back of the cardboard: the cracked, yellow masking tape confirmed his suspicion. The sign had been there for a very long time.

Will then took a closer look at the elevator. The door seemed smaller than other elevator doors he had seen. "Maybe it's because the rest of the store is so large," he said to himself.

He noticed that the faceplate was off of the call box and that the "Down" button was missing.

He tried to replace the sign. It wouldn't stick: the tape was too old. He set the sign on the floor to the right of the elevator and turned to leave. On an impulse he turned back and pressed the "Up" button.

Nothing happened.

"That was a dumb thing to do," Will said, under his breath. He started to leave. He was just heading around the boxes when he heard the soft 'ding' of a bell and the sliding of a door.

He turned back. The elevator door was open! A warm, fluorescent light shone out of it.

Will took a few cautious steps back towards the elevator and peered inside.

"Hello, there!" said a cheery voice.

Will jumped back in surprise. Just inside the elevator door, on the left side, was a young man in his mid-twenties wearing a maroon uniform with gold buttons on the jacket and gold stripes on the sides of his pants legs. He was also wearing a maroon cap with gold stripes on it.

"Did you call for the elevator?" the man asked.

Will said nothing as he stared at the man.

"Excuse me, but did you call for the elevator?" the man repeated.

Will finally found his voice. "I thought the elevator was out of order," he stammered.

The man smiled. "If it was out of order, then why did you press the button?"

Will ignored the question. "Is this a magic elevator?" he asked.

"No," the man said, "it's an Otis."

"A what?" asked a puzzled Will.

The man laughed. "That's just a little elevator humor. Otis is the name of the manufacturer. And, no, this is not a magic elevator. The people who used to own the store hired me to run the elevator for any of the old employees who wanted to take a last look at the place. You seem a little too young to have worked here. Who are you?"

"My name is Will," he said, still not quite recovered from the shock. "I'm here with my great grandmother. She used to work here."

The elevator operator poked his head out and looked around. "I don't see anybody else with you," he said with a grin.

"She's talking with some friends out in the front of the store. I was just doing some exploring."

"Well," said the operator, "I can certainly help you with that. There are three other floors and a basement at your disposal. Come on in. My name is Max. It is a pleasure to meet you, Will. Where would you like to go?"

Will stepped into the elevator and looked around. It seemed normal enough. The walls were painted a clean, pale yellow. Bright fluorescent lights shone overhead. And he had not been mistaken: it *was* a very small elevator. Max sensed Will's unasked question.

"Total capacity of 6 passengers," he said. "That includes the operator."

"Six people aren't much of a load," Will noted.

"True," Max nodded in agreement, "but The Hub management believed in creating a warm, intimate atmosphere. A small elevator, with a uniformed operator inside, created the impression that it was your own private elevator. That really didn't create a problem of forcing people to wait for the next car. Believe it or not, most people preferred taking the stairs back in the day. At any rate, here you are: so where would you like to go, Will?"

Will thought for a moment. He remembered what Gigi had had told him about the great Christmases at the store and her fond memories of the people she worked with.

"Fourth floor, please," he said.

"Fourth floor coming up," said Max as he pushed to button to close the door.

CHAPTER TEN

There was a gentle bump as the elevator started upward. Will steadied himself against the metal railing that ran around the inside of the car.

"So, the company hired you to run this elevator just for this one day?" he asked Max.

"Just for today," Max replied. "Fortunately, I have other work."

"What do you do?" Will asked.

Max smiled, "It's kind of hard to describe," he said. "I'm part personal assistant and part factory worker."

"What do you make?"

"Oh," said Max, casually, "just stuff."

"What kind of stuff?" pressed Will.

There was another bump and the soft 'ding' of the bell.

"We're here," Max announced as the door opened. "Welcome to the fourth floor!"

A blast of warm, humid air hit Will full in the face. It carried with it a strong odor.

"Wow," said Will, holding his nose, "it really stinks up here!"

"You have to expect that," Max explained. "No one has been up here for almost 25 years. There has been no heat or air conditioning on this floor for almost a quarter of a century. There is water damage from a leaky roof. We've got mold and mildew: you name it, we've got it! We probably have a pretty healthy batch of spiders and rats up here as well, so watch your step! The bad smell comes from rotting carpet. Fortunately, some workers came up here earlier in the day and opened up some windows. That should help a little bit."

"It doesn't help very much!" Will said, still holding his nose.

"We don't have to stay here," Max offered. "I can take you to one of the other floors. I can even take you to the basement. I have to warn you, though: I was down in the basement earlier and it is out-of-this-world bad!"

Will shook his head. "No, I think I'll look around up here."

"Suit yourself," said Max. "Just remember: when you are done, just come back to the elevator and hit the button. I'll come back for you."

Will nodded, "That sounds good to me. I can't imagine that I'll be up here very long."

With that, he stepped out onto the fourth floor. He heard the door of the elevator slide shut behind him.

Will took a few moments to take in his surroundings. The fourth floor was very different from the ground floor. For one thing, the ceiling was only about 10 feet high. Instead of the 'open' feeling created by the first floor columns, a series of walls divided the fourth floor into a veritable maze complete with narrow passageways. Despite the lack of electricity, the room was surprisingly well-lit, owing to the fact that several large windows were located on each of the four outer walls. These windows, however, were of a curious construction. Instead of plate glass, the builders had used glass blocks. Each block was a square, roughly 10 inches by 10 inches and about 4 inches thick. Each window on the floor was a rectangle 8 blocks high by 4 blocks wide.

Rot was everywhere: falling plaster, peeling paint, decomposing carpet and shredded wallpaper were all that remained of The Hub's fourth floor. Water from the roof dripped through a gaping hole in the ceiling off to Will's right. He took a step in that direction and his tennis shoe slipped on the wet, slimy carpet.

"I don't think I'll explore up here after all," Will said out loud. "Gigi might have loved this floor in her day, but it sure is a dump now! I think I'll check out the other floors."

With that, Will turned and pressed the "Down" button and waited for Max to return. He waited and he waited: no elevator. He pressed the button again, several times. Still, no elevator came. He placed an ear against the elevator door and listened for the sound of the returning car. He heard nothing.

"That's weird," said a very puzzled Will. "Max said all I had to do was press the button. I guess I'm going to have to find the stairs."

Will did not want to slog through the soggy carpet on his right, so he turned left and began walking along the wall on that side. He remembered that the stairway was located on the north side of the store. The route required him to walk halfway around the floor.

Thankfully, the floor in the direction he was walking was in reasonably good shape. Will still had to pick his way through paint and plaster chips and step around an old light fixture that had fallen from the ceiling. He passed several walls that divided the floor into aisle ways. Wooden shelves were permanently affixed to these walls: shelves that had stood empty now for almost a quarter of a century.

He came to the west wall and turned right (so as to head north), and suddenly stopped.

About 50 feet ahead of him, looking out of a gap in one of the windows, was a man. He was an older man, probably in his late seventies, about six feet tall, with a medium build and short, white hair. He was wearing a short-sleeved red and gray checkered shirt and dark blue work pants. Will would have assumed the man was a workman: except for the fact that he seemed a bit too old to be a worker; additionally, he didn't have any tools. On top of that, he wasn't doing anything except looking out the window.

Will must have gasped, or made a noise of some sort, because the man turned to face him.

"Well, hello there young fellow," he said in a kind, welcoming voice. "What brings you to a dump like this?"

"I'm here with my great-grandmother," said Will, not moving any closer. "She used to work at this store. She's downstairs at the reunion."

The man nodded. "I used to work here myself, at least part-time. I did seasonal work here."

"What kind of seasonal work?" Will asked, maintaining his position at the end of the aisle.

"I worked as the store Santa Claus for several years," the man replied.

"Really?" said Will, walking towards the man. "Gigi said that Christmases here were pretty special."

"Who is Gigi?" the man asked.

"Gigi is my great-grandmother," Will replied.

"Well, she was right about that," the old man said. "You couldn't find a more exciting place than this floor for those four weeks between Thanksgiving and Christmas. It was a magical place, that's for certain." He turned to look out the window again before adding, softly, "I really miss it."

By now, Will had reached the place where the man stood. The window was like the rest of the windows on this floor, except that several of the glass blocks had been carefully removed. This afforded a clear view of the impoverished city.

"It didn't use to be like this," the man said as he continued to stare out the window. "There used to be a living city out there: cars, buses, businesses, noise and people. There used to be lots and lots of people. Now look at it: it's a veritable ghost town."

Will could sense sadness in the man's voice and it made him uneasy. He decided to change the subject. "What happened to the glass blocks in this window?" he asked.

The man turned to face him, "The management of the store wanted to do something special for their old employees. Every person who comes to the reunion today will put their name and address on a sheet of paper. In several weeks they will receive a package. Inside that package will be one of these window blocks. An artist is going to etch a picture of the Hub on one side of the glass. When the light shines through, it will look like the old store all lit up again. It isn't much, but it's a nice gesture. By the way, you and I haven't been properly introduced. My name is Daniel: Daniel Turner."

"My name is Will Fellows."

"Well, pleased to meet you, Will," said Daniel, shaking the boy's hand, warmly. "Have you done much exploring here today?"

"Not a whole lot," Will admitted. "I looked around the first floor and then I came up here. What have you been doing?"

"Oh, I bypassed the reunion," Daniel said. "I liked the people I worked with, that's for sure; but, I guess I was more interested in coming up here and looking at my old work area. I took the stairs."

There was an awkward moment of silence before Will said, "The fourth floor doesn't quite look like it used to, does it?"

Daniel laughed, "No, Will, it doesn't. In fact, I would probably be hard-pressed to know exactly where it was that we set up the old toy land. Still, it might be fun to try and find out. Would you care to tag along?"

Will glanced briefly at his cell phone, there was still quite a bit of time left before he was due to meet up with Gigi. "Sure," he said to Daniel, "let's go take a look!"

The two of them picked their way along the rubble-strewn aisle until they reached the north wall. The stairway was almost directly in front of them. They turned right and walked about 30 feet. Daniel then stopped and pointed off to his right. "Do you see this open area, here?" he asked Will. "If I am not mistaken, this is where we set up Santa's Toyland. There was a little, lighted archway right here where the kids would line up. They would come over to this spot where Santa's throne was, get their picture taken with Santa, and then head off that way to get a treat. The whole floor was decorated like you wouldn't believe. There were miniature train displays and toys of every size, shape and description!"

"I would have loved to have seen it," Will said.

"I wonder," said Daniel, his voice trailing off into silence. He began walking towards small door on the north wall.

"What?" asked Will, "what do you wonder?"

Daniel kept walking towards the door, but called back over his shoulder. "This used to be the storage room where we kept Santa's throne. I wonder if it is still here?"

"I doubt it," Will said, skeptically, "I mean, they took everything else out of the store. Why would they leave that?"

Daniel reached the door and put his hand on the knob. He turned back to face Will. "There's no logical reason to believe that they would leave it. But then again, there isn't much everyday demand for a throne, so you never know." He tried the knob: the door was locked.

Daniel turned to face Will. "Considering the current state of the building, I don't suppose I would get in too much trouble if I did this." With that, Daniel kicked in the storeroom door. The wood gave way with a loud 'crack!'

"That felt good," Daniel said with satisfaction. He peered inside. "It's pretty dark in there," he said, "I don't think we'll be able to find anything."

"Maybe this will help," said Will, digging into his pocket. He produced his cellphone. "I have a flashlight app on my phone. Let's see if that helps." In a matter of moments, the phone was emitting a bright rectangle of light. He handed the phone to Daniel.

"Thank you, kindly," said Daniel, as he stepped into the room. Will followed.

The storeroom was relatively small: roughly 8 feet by 10 feet and the same height as the rest of the fourth floor. Will was surprised to find that the room was still packed with a number of items. He was not surprised that the storeroom smelled as bad as the rest of the floor.

"Jackpot!" Daniel shouted. At the far end of the room, on the left-hand side, was a lumpy form wrapped with a heavy canvas. "Help me lug this thing out, Will!"

Removing the chair from the storeroom was not an easy task. First, they had to move several large items, including a massive, ancient vacuum cleaner, out into the store. The throne proved to be quite heavy and it took both Will and

Daniel, each using both hands, to move it. This meant that they could not hold the cell phone flashlight. Daniel set it down so that the beam bounced back weakly from the heavily-mildewed ceiling. Huffing and puffing, the two were eventually able to lug the throne out to the place where Daniel said it was supposed to go.

"Better get your cell phone while I catch my breath," Daniel said. Will dutifully went back to the storeroom and returned a few seconds later.

"Let's have a look at her," Daniel said, as he removed the heavy canvas.

Will drew in a sharp breath: the cover had done an incredible job of protecting the chair. The throne was in nearly perfect condition. It was a wooden chair, stained dark brown, with a back about 5 feet high. The seat and back cushions were made of soft, rich, red velvet. The arm rests of the chair were curved at the ends and there were exquisite carvings all over the woodwork. The carvings were highlighted in bright gold leaf.

"Holy cow!" exclaimed Will. "Look at this thing! I can't believe it's been sitting here all this time and it looks this good!"

"She is a beauty," admitted Daniel, admiringly. "Why don't you try it out?"

"You mean sit in it?" Will asked.

"Why not?" Daniel said, with a hearty laugh. "It is a chair, isn't it? Give it a try!"

Very gently, Will eased himself onto the chair. He sank comfortably into the luxurious, soft velvet and leaned back against its cushion. His hands curled around the cool curves at the end of the arm rests. A sweet, rich smell rose from the chair. But how could that be? Everything else in the store smelled of rot and decay!

Daniel saw the puzzled look on Will's face and answered his unasked question. "It's made of cedar," he said. "Cedar retains its smell for a long, long time."

Will closed his eyes and settled even further into the chair's soft embrace. Never had he sat in a chair such as this!

"Now you see why I liked it so much," said Daniel softly.

"I bet it's cool being a store Santa," Will said, his eyes still shut.

"Indeed it is," admitted Daniel.

"What was it like?" asked Will, unwilling to open his eyes as he reveled in the chair's comfort.

"Well," began Daniel, "First try to imagine the weather outside the store. It's eight o'clock on Friday night, one week before Christmas. It is snowing. There are already 4 inches of snow on the ground and it is still coming down hard. The streets are a mess, but they are nevertheless crowded with holiday shoppers. Despite the weather, or maybe because of it, everyone is in a festive mood! Shoppers stream into The Hub. Just inside the main entrance is a 15-foot, live tree decked out with gold ornaments and bright red ribbon. A choir from one of the local high schools performs their Christmas concert in front of the tree.

"On every floor there are greeters whose only job is to wish customers a Merry Christmas and hand out candy canes to them. And, on every floor there are signs that say, 'Visit Santa and his Toyland on the fourth floor.'

"Meanwhile, on the fourth floor, there is magic everywhere! There are Christmas lights everywhere you look —and not those silly LED lights you see nowadays: no, these are the big C9 bulbs. There are bubble lights and twinkly lights. There's Christmas music by all the great artists: Bing Crosby, Nat King Cole, Frank Sinatra, and Rosemary Clooney. The shelves are stocked with toys of every description.   There is a model train display with an engine that puffs out real smoke!

"And finally, there is Santa himself: sitting in that very chair!   Imagine all the excited little boys and girls climbing into your lap to whisper in your ear what they want for Christmas and telling you how good they have been all year. Imagine them hopping down off your lap and running over to get their small gift along with a fresh-baked cookie and some hot chocolate."

Will smiled.   He could easily imagine it all.   He could visualize the store in all its glory.   He could even hear the music and smell the goodies.

Suddenly, he sat bolt upright in the chair.   Although his eyes remained closed, Will realized, with alarm, that he wasn't just imagining the sounds and the smells: he was actually hearing and smelling them!

Cautiously, he opened one eye: then both eyes flew wide open.   The fourth floor was no longer the decaying corpse of a long-dead department store: it had been transformed into the very scene Daniel had been describing!

Will whirled around to face Daniel.

"Surprise," Daniel said, softly.

"Hey!   Wait a minute!" said Will in shocked disbelief as he stared at the man in the red suit.   "You're ..."

"Yeah," admitted Daniel, sheepishly.   "I'm Santa Claus."

CHAPTER ELEVEN

Will tried to rise from the chair, but found that his legs would not support him.

"Whoa, there, chief," Daniel cautioned him. "Wait a minute or two: sometimes a sudden shock to the mind affects the body as well. Just relax."

"Are you really Santa Claus?" Will asked weakly.

"Who else would go around dressed like this in June?" Daniel replied wryly.

"But, why are you here, in this junk pile?" Will asked, still in a stupor.

Daniel grinned. "I told you: I used to work here. I was the store Santa for 17 years."

"But, why would the real Santa Claus work as a store Santa?"

This time Daniel laughed out loud. "It started out as a joke, really. Someone sent me a newspaper clipping that said The Hub was going to have the 'real' Santa Claus in their store following the annual Christmas parade. I hate it when people lie, so I decided to make certain that the store got the genuine article. I turned operations at the North Pole over to my personal assistant and slipped into town. I found the guy the store originally hired and slipped him a hundred bucks to let me take over. And, you know what? I had a blast! It was great to get out of the shop for a while and mingle with the people! I came back for the next 16 years in a row. I would have done it longer, had things not changed."

"They closed the store, right?" Will guessed.

"No, the store went on for another 30 years after I quit. No, it was something else that made me give up the gig."

"What happened?" Will asked, earnestly.

"I prefer not to talk about it," Daniel said softly.

"Come on, Daniel—I mean, Santa. You always tell us kids to talk to you: why don't you trust one of us for a change?"

Daniel turned away from Will and bowed his head. In a voice that was barely audible he said, "I got my heart broken."

"You?" exclaimed Will in a voice that was much louder than he intended.

"Why not me?" asked Daniel as he turned back to face the boy. "I'm human, too. You've watched too many Christmas specials if you think Santa is a 'jolly old elf' all the time. The truth of the matter is, a girl broke my heart."

Will was puzzled. "You mean a little girl broke your heart?"

Daniel rolled his eyes. "No, Will: I mean a big girl, a woman, broke my heart. She was one of the employees here at the store."

"Santa Claus dated a girl here at The Hub?" wondered Will, in amazement.

Daniel sighed audibly. "No, Will. I didn't date a girl here at The Hub. I wanted to date her. But, I was too shy to even talk to her."

Will was unable to stifle a laugh. "You were too shy to ask a girl out? You're one of the most famous people in the world! You go into practically everyone's house!"

"Right," Daniel said, nodding in agreement. "And when do I go? In the middle of the night after everyone has gone to bed! The whole world thinks that I do that because I want the gifts to be a surprise. I do it so I don't have to run into people and be forced into awkward conversations."

"But you talk to millions of kids," Will argued.

"That's right," Daniel shot back. "I talk to *kids:* and, by now, its *billions* of kids if you want to be accurate. But, let those kids grow up and become adults and I get shy. Let them grow up and become women and I get absolutely tongue-tied." Daniel turned away again and faced the wall.

Will thought very carefully before he spoke again. "What kind of girl was she?" he asked gently.

Daniel shrugged, but did not turn around when he answered. "She was kind, beautiful, witty and smart. I couldn't wait to get to work each day just so I could catch a glimpse of her. I made a gift for her in the little hotel room where I was staying. It was a music box. I figured if she liked it, maybe she would like me and go out with me."

"Did she like the music box?" asked Will, quietly.

Daniel shook his head. "I never even gave it to her: I was too shy." For a moment, Daniel said nothing. Then, he reached into the right hand pocket of his Santa coat. "Would you believe I've carried it with me all of these years?" He withdrew his hand: in it he held a small silver box, exquisitely crafted. He opened it, and the sweetest tune Will had ever heard began to play. As it played, Daniel softly sang:

"Through summer's heat or winter's chill
mid falling leaves or daffodils

though cruel time our bodies bend
my love for you will know no end."

Daniel closed the box and returned it to his pocket. He bowed his head. Will wasn't sure, but he thought he heard a muffled sob. Almost as an afterthought he asked, "What was her name, Santa?"

"Edna. Edna Perry."

Will turned pale and gasped, "Gigi!"

"Gigi, what?" asked Daniel, as he turned around.

"Not 'Gigi, what'," Will corrected, "Gigi who! Gigi is the nickname I gave to my great-grandmother: it stands for the initials G.G.; you know—great-grandma? But her maiden name was Edna Perry! You had a crush on my great-grandma!"

Now it was Daniel's turn to be incredulous. "Are you serious?"

Will frowned. "Are you sure you're Santa Claus? I thought you knew who everybody was!"

Daniel held up his hand to stop Will. "I told you already: I restrict myself to kids. Once they grow up, they tend to drop off my radar. Edna dropped off my radar the day Charles showed up."

"Do you mean my great-grandpa, Chuck?" Will asked.

Daniel's shoulders sagged. "I suppose that's who I mean. How is he doing?"

"He died when I was five years old," Will said, simply.

"Really?" Daniel asked, brightening considerably. Then, realizing how callous that sounded, he added more soberly, "I'm sorry, Will."

Will grinned. "That's OK, Santa. The point is, she's available now. And, she's downstairs! Why don't you come down with me and see her?"

Daniel held up both hands and shook his head. "No, I couldn't do that!"

"Why couldn't you?" Will demanded, hands on his hips.

"I'd be too nervous to talk to her," Daniel stammered.

"Fine!" said Will as he strode off. "If you won't go down to see Gigi, I'll just bring her up here!"

"Wait!" Daniel shouted, running after the boy, "you can't do that!"

"Why can't I?" countered Will.

"What are you going to say to her? 'Come with me, Gigi —Santa Claus is upstairs and he wants to ask you to go to the movies with him?' They'll lock, you up for being a nut, boy!"

Will walked back until he was nose to nose with Daniel. "Listen, Santa: I am going to get Gigi up here somehow. You just promise to be here when I get back. Do you understand?"

Something in Will's tone made Daniel back down. Meekly, he replied, "I'll be here. I promise."

"Good!" said Will firmly. "Now, I need to get to the stairs."

"It would be faster to take the elevator," Daniel reminded him.

"The elevator isn't working," Will countered. "I tried to get it to come back up here for a full 5 minutes and I couldn't even hear the stupid thing running."

Daniel took him by the arm. "Let's give it another try: I have a feeling it will work this time."

The two of them walked briskly through the brightly decorated fourth floor. They walked past lighted trees, mountains of gaily-wrapped packages and shelves bulging with toys. Will was too excited to notice any of it.

They arrived at the elevator. Daniel pressed the "Down" button. Immediately, the door opened.

"Good evening, Boss!" Max called cheerfully.

"Good evening, Max!" Daniel said with a smile.

"You two know each other?" Will asked, with wonder.

"We should know each other," answered Max. "I've worked as his personal assistant for the past 85 years!"

"Meet my head elf," Daniel said with a broad grin.

"What do you mean 'head elf'?" Will demanded. "The guy is almost 6 feet tall!"

"Elves come in all sizes," explained Daniel. "We like to promote the short ones because they look cuter on the Christmas cards. Max? Take this young man back to the first floor and wait for him: he should be back in a matter of moments with a passenger in tow."

"Will do, Boss!" Max answered with a snappy salute. He reached for the first floor button, but Will grabbed his arm.

"You swear to be here when we get back, Santa?" he asked solemnly.

"I promise," Daniel answered. "I won't move from this spot."

Will nodded. "OK, Max: let's get going!"

CHAPTER TWELVE

Will's mind was racing as the elevator began its descent. What could he possibly say to Gigi to get her to follow him upstairs? Like Daniel had said, he couldn't very well tell her that Santa Claus was upstairs waiting to ask her out on a date! And. there was another concern: a quick look at his cell phone informed Will that it was now 3:30. There were only 45 minutes left until he and Gigi had to get ready to meet their bus!

A gentle bump let Will know they had reached the ground floor.

The door opened and Will stepped out. He heard the door slide shut behind him. He crept to the end of the pile of boxes and carefully peered around the corner. There was no one else in sight. Briskly, he set off for the reunion area.

He had to weave his way through the furniture store. He was encouraged to find that the sale was winding down and there were not many customers left. He was equally excited to find the Hub celebration drawing to a close. Only about 10 former employees remained. Gigi was seated at a round table, talking to the same two co-workers Will had left her with. They were involved in a spirited conversation when he arrived at their table.

"Seriously, Martha," Gigi was saying, "you never heard such carrying on in your life! When Simmons accidentally hit that 500 gallon fish tank with the stepladder it sent water and tropical fish everywhere! They had to close the Housewares department for three days while they cleaned up the mess!"

The three ladies roared with laughter.

Will tried to catch Gigi's attention, but he did not want to be rude and interrupt the conversation: he had been taught to always be polite. Fortunately, Gigi looked up to see him shifting uncomfortably from foot to foot.

"Sweetheart," she said, "if you need to use the restroom, it's over by the furniture check-out."

"What?" asked Will, puzzled. Then, recovering, he said, "No, Gigi, I'm fine. But I do need to ask you something."

"What is it, luv?" she asked, looking up at him.

"Actually, I need you to come with me to look at something," he said, sounding far more nervous than he intended.

"Can it wait a few minutes?" Gigi asked. "Martha and Eloise have to leave shortly and I want to spend more time with them."

"It's kind of important," Will said, urgently.

"What is it you want me to see?" Gigi asked patiently.

"I'd really rather not say, if you don't mind," Will said, nervously.

"Oh, you can talk around us," said Eloise with a laugh. "We don't get embarrassed easily!"

"Oh, it's nothing like that," Will said, holding up both hands. "I just want to show Gigi something privately."

"Go ahead and go with the boy," Martha said, patting Gigi on the arm. "A few minutes aren't going to make that much difference. If we had the rest of the week we still wouldn't have enough time to catch up on old times. We'll stick around for another 15 minutes or so: if you are back by then, fine; if not, you have our phone numbers."

Gigi smiled fondly at her two friends. "Thank you, girls," she said, earnestly. "It's been great seeing you again. Take care of yourselves!" She then gave each of them a hug.

"All right, Will," she said, taking his arm. "Show me what is so earth-shatteringly important."

Wordlessly, Will began leading Gigi through the furniture store towards the store's east wall.

"Where are we going?" Gigi finally asked him.

"Um, I found something really cool up on that mezzanine you told me about," Will lied.

"The mezzanine is on the north wall," Gigi reminded him, gently.

Will did not answer her. He glanced around quickly to make sure no one was following them. Suddenly, he steered Gigi toward the stack of boxes. "This way!" he said, under his breath.

"Where are we going?" Gigi asked, concern in her voice.

"Keep your voice down and follow me," Will whispered. Obediently, Gigi followed him around the boxes. In seconds they were at the elevator.

"Here we are," Will said breathlessly.

Gigi stared at him. "You dragged me away from my two best friends in the whole world to show me a broken down elevator?" she asked, incredulously. "What is wrong with you, boy?"

Will ignored the question. "Push the button, Gigi," he said.

"Will," she said, "this elevator has not run for years! There's a sign here that says, 'Out of order'! The 'Down' button is gone!"

"Push the other button," Will told her.

"Will, this is nonsense! I'm going back to my friends!" Gigi started to leave, but Will gently put a hand on her shoulder.

"Gigi, I know this doesn't make sense. But, think for a minute: have I ever asked you to do anything that would embarrass you or make you look stupid?"

"No, you haven't," Gigi admitted.

"Then, I won't do it now," Will said firmly. "Just trust me and press the button."

Edna shook her head as she looked at her great-grandson. "You are a mystery sometimes, child. But, if you insist ..." Her voice trailed off as she stepped forward and pressed "Up".

Instantly, with a soft 'ding', the door opened.

"Good afternoon, you two," said the smiling elevator operator.

Gigi's mouth dropped open in amazement. After a moment or two she whispered, "Max? Is that you?"

Will turned to face his great-grandmother. "You know him?" he asked in surprise.

"I *knew* him," she said as if in a trance, "almost 60 years ago, when I worked here. He hasn't aged a day! How is that possible?"

Max reached out and helped Will guide Gigi into the car. "I think things will become pretty clear in a minute," he said. He pressed the button and closed the door.

"Where are we going?" she asked Will, still in a daze.

Will grinned at her, "We're going to the fourth floor. There's someone there who wants to see you."

"Who wants to see me?" Gigi asked, still not quite regaining her composure.

"You'll see," Will said, with a broad smile.

They rode wordlessly for the next ten seconds. The car gently lurched to a stop and the door opened. There was the fourth floor, gloriously restored to its Christmas splendor. And there, also, was a gentle man in a Santa suit: his hat respectfully removed in the presence of a lady.

"Hello, Edna," the man meekly said. "Do you remember me?"

Gigi, holding tightly to Will's hand, stepped forward and looked deep into the stranger's eyes. After a moment, she whispered, "Daniel? Is that you?"

A broad smile slowly spread across Daniel's face. "Welcome back, Edna," he said softly.

Gigi looked past Daniel to the glittering showroom. "How on earth?" she murmured.

"He's not just a store Santa, Gigi," Will said, beaming. "He's the real deal! And, you know what? He's had a crush on you all these years!"

Gigi turned to face Daniel. "Is that true?" she asked.

Daniel's face turned as red as the rest of his suit. He looked at the floor as he stammered, "Yes, it's true."

"We worked together all of those years and yet you never said a word about how you felt," Gigi said quietly. "Why?"

Daniel continued to look at the floor. "I didn't know what to say. You were so beautiful and smart. And then Charles came along. I guess I just didn't know how to ..." his voice drifted off into silence.

Gigi stepped forward and tenderly placed her right hand on Daniel's cheek. "You silly man," she said quietly. "You dear, sweet, silly man. Didn't you ever notice how often I glanced your way? How admiringly I watched as you dealt with that endless stream of children? I never saw a sweeter, kinder man. If you would have just spoken to me I'd have been yours in a heartbeat."

Daniel raised his head, but his eyes were still filled with sadness. "I guess I blew my chance, didn't I?"

Gigi smiled, "You certainly did back then, but here we are now. I'm free again; that is, if you are still interested."

A wide grin spread across Daniel's face. "I am most certainly still interested! Would you care to take a walk down memory lane?" He gestured to the brightly festooned fourth floor.

"I would love it!" Gigi said, taking his arm. The two of them started off, then Gigi turned back and said, "Will, I forgot my purse downstairs. Would you mind retrieving it for me?"

"I'd be glad to," Will said, "if Max will take me back down."

"Your wish is my command," said Max with a deep bow.

"We'll be right back!" announced Will, as he pushed the first floor button himself.

CHAPTER THIRTEEN

Will was relieved to find that Gigi's two friends were still at the reunion. "Excuse me," he said to Eloise, "my great-grandmother said she left her purse here. May I have it, please?"

"I have it with me," said Martha. "I tried calling after you, when you first left, but you apparently didn't hear me. I take it that Edna won't be coming back to join us?"

Will shook his head, "I don't think so: she ran into another old friend and is busy talking with him."

"Well, be sure and tell her again how much fun we had today. Remind her to call us, soon!" Eloise said.

"I will do that," Will promised, as he sprinted off for the elevator. He was back to the box pile in a matter of moments. He had just ducked behind the pile and was about to push the "Up" button when heard a man bark, sharply, "What are you doing back here?"

Will turned to see a large, scowling security guard glaring at him.

"I asked you what you're doing here," the man repeated.

"I was just taking my great-grandma's purse back to her," Will stammered.

The guard sneered at him. "Are you sure you didn't *steal* that purse from somebody?"

"No, I didn't steal it!" Will said, adamantly. "I told you: I'm taking this purse up to my great-grandmother. She's on the fourth floor."

"There are a couple of things wrong with your story," the guard said, menacingly. "First of all, no one is permitted anywhere in the store except this ground floor. Secondly, even if they were allowed, they aren't going anywhere on that thing: it's broken!" The man jabbed a finger in the direction of the elevator.

"That's not true," Will said, defiantly. "I've ridden this elevator four times already today!"

"I know you're a liar now, kid" the guard said, advancing towards Will. "That elevator hasn't run in years and I can prove it!" He reached for a panel just above the elevator door and slid it to one side. "Take a look!" he commanded Will.

Will stared up in wide-eyed horror.

The elevator's cable was frayed and broken.

CHAPTER FOURTEEN

"You're coming with me!" the guard snarled as he reached for Will.

Will whirled around and began running as fast as his legs would carry him, the purse still clutched in his hands. "Get back here!" he heard the guard bellow after him.

The stairs, I've got to get to the stairs! Will thought to himself as he dashed wildly through the store. He could hear the heavy footsteps of the guard running after him.

Will reached the stairs and sprinted up them. He had no time to admire their former beauty, no chance to appreciate the loving craftsmanship that had gone into their construction: this was a frantic dash to the fourth floor. He could hear the guard climbing the stairs behind him: the man was large and slow, but he was still coming!

Will passed the second and third floors. "Gigi! Daniel! Max! Somebody, anybody, help me!" he panted as he doggedly continued up the steps. One more flight and he burst through the double doors onto the fourth floor.

It was a decaying, desolate wasteland.

Will stared, mouth agape. Suddenly, he heard the unsteady steps of the security guard plodding closer and closer.   He quickly moved away from the stairway.   A few moments later, the pale, staggering guard appeared.

"Hold it right there, kid!" the guard panted, hands on his knees.

"I told you, I didn't steal this purse!" Will said, emphatically.   "This belongs to my great-grandmother, Edna Black.   She's up here on this floor: I can prove it to you!"

The guard reached for a walkie-talkie on his belt.   "I've got a suspected purse snatcher on the fourth floor!   I need assistance on the fourth floor, stat!"   He looked at Will. "OK, kid.   I have help coming.   There is nowhere for you to go.   If you get past me, they'll catch you on the stairs.   If you have proof your great-grandma is up here, you better show it to me now!"

"Alright," Will said, nervously.   "I was up here earlier and ran into an old guy named Daniel Turner.   He said he used to be a store Santa years ago here at The Hub.   He even showed me the throne he used to use as Santa.   It's magnificent, and its right over here!   Follow me!"

The guard, still worn out from his climb, began walking unsteadily towards Will.   "This better not be a trick, kid," he wheezed.

"It isn't any trick," Will assured him.   "It's just around the corner here."   Will took a few more steps, then stopped in his tracks.   The purse dropped from his hands.

There, in the middle of the floor, was Santa's throne. The wood was warped and cracked; the velvet cushions white with mildew.   Will slumped to his knees.

The guard was at Will's side in a matter of seconds.   "So this is Santa's glorious throne, eh?" he sneered as he dragged Will to his feet.   He was reaching for his pair of handcuffs when they both heard it: the clear, unmistakable 'ding' of a bell and the sliding of an elevator door.

This was followed by the sound of a young woman's laugh and the sweet tinkling of a music box. Then, they heard the clear strong voice of a young man, singing:

> *"Through summer's heat or winter's chill*
> *mid falling leaves or daffodils*
> *though cruel time our bodies bend*
> *my love for you will know no end."*

CHAPTER FIFTEEN

"Not another word out of you, young man! We will discuss this when we get home!"

Will settled back wearily into the back seat of the family car. It had been a long night. The police had detained him at The Hub till 9:00 pm, pummeling him with questions. His parents had been summoned to the store (his Dad from work, his Mom from her Card Club).

Neither of his parents believed his story. Will couldn't blame them: how do you convince someone that your great-grandmother just ran off with Santa Claus?

The interrogation had been the worst thing. To be fair, the security guard had been truthful, ("I swear to you, I heard the elevator. I heard the music box. And, I heard both a man and a woman's voice!") Still, there was only one exit from the fourth floor: that was the staircase, and 3 city policemen swore that no one had gotten past them on the stairs.

A thorough search of the building was conducted, but there was no sign of Gigi or of anyone matching the descriptions of Daniel or Max. The police told Will's parents that a missing person's report would be filed and they released Will into their custody.

It was Will's mother who told him to be quiet until they got home.

The clock read 9:45 pm when Will and his folks walked through the front door.

"Go to your room," his mother said. "Once your Father and I have talked, we'll call you down and tell you what we have decided to do."

Wordlessly, Will started up the stairs.

"I need a drink," Will's father said as he headed into the kitchen. A moment later they heard him cry out, "Linda! Will! Get in here!"

Will and his mother ran to the kitchen. Will's father was standing at the kitchen counter, white as a sheet, holding a piece of paper from a yellow legal pad. "Listen to this," he said.

"'My dearest family,'" he read from the letter, "'I am so sorry we missed you. Daniel and I just stopped by for a few minutes to pick up some of my things. It has been quite a day, as I'm sure Will has told you. There won't be any need for the assisted living center now: I've got a new place to live. Don't be alarmed when you see my medications on the counter: Daniel assures me that I won't require them anymore. We promise to drop in and see you when we can, although you need to understand that our schedule is going to be quite full. Take care and know that we love you. All my love, Gigi. P.S. The gift on the table is for all of you'."

Will looked and saw a large, brightly-wrapped package on the kitchen table.

"Go ahead and open it," his mother said, softly.

Will carefully untied the ribbon and opened the wrapping paper. Inside the box, wrapped in tissue paper, was one of the glass blocks from The Hub. A beautiful red ribbon ran around the outer edge of the block.   The front of the block was covered with a dark film of some kind.   Etched into the film were the figures of Gigi, Daniel and Max standing before the open door of a store elevator.   Below the etching were the words, *"All our love, forever and al*ways."

About the Author

Bill Hunt lives in Ohio with his wife Linda, where he has been the minister of the Rosehill Church of Christ in Reynoldsburg since 1992. They have two married daughters.

He is the author of the *Garson the Dragon* series, and the Crimon Short story *One Bright Night*.

Coming soon, Garson the Illustrated series. Keep your eye on the first of these books coming in 2016.

https://www.facebook.com/pages/Garson/1510374865881162
http://www.garsonbooks.com/
On Smashwords
https://www.smashwords.com/books/view/488815
Print Version: https://www.createspace.com/5051814
http://crimsoncloakpublishing.com/bill-hunt_2.html

http://crimsoncloakpublishing.com